Compact of Fire

A Censored City Novelette

MELANIE HARDING-SHAW

The author acknowledges the excerpt quoted from 'Venus and Adonis' by William Shakespeare. 'Venus and Adonis' was first published in 1593.

Publisher:
https://www.melaniehardingshaw.com/

CENSORED CITY NOVELETTES

Would She Be Gone

Compact of Fire

Hell is Empty

CONTENTS

CHAPTER 1

Sera gripped her phone with stiff fingers and forced herself to shorten her strides so Secretary for Literary Safety Brenton Turnstin could keep up. She hated it when he tried to play power-games with the press by keeping them waiting.

"What can I say about the investigation, again?" Brenton asked.

Sera breathed deep to calm herself. If he'd read her brief, he wouldn't have needed to ask. "It's an active investigation. No comment. Push the hashtag and the tip-off number."

"Right. What have I got on after this?"

"You cleared your schedule. And your wife left a message at lunchtime to call her."

He paused at the door to the press conference room and turned towards her, smiling. "What would I do without you?" He leaned forward and kissed her lips, pushing her back against the cool wall.

For a moment, Sera forgot where they were and kissed him back. Then she pushed him away, her panicked eyes searching the thankfully empty corridor for anyone that might see them. Her chest fluttered with that same old feeling of excitement and shame.

"Stop that, Bren. You need to focus," she whispered, out of breath.

He grinned again, kissed her one more time just to show he could, and then pushed the door open. The noise of journalists talking and rustling washed out into the hallway before cutting off abruptly as they realised the main act had arrived.

Sera stood off to the side, out of camera shot and watched Bren step up to the podium like he owned it.

"Good Afternoon. As you are aware, a former police officer has allegedly betrayed our country and put millions at risk by interfering with the Librarian algorithm."

Sera kept her face carefully relaxed. What part of "no comment" had he not understood?

"I can assure you, our law enforcement agencies are working tirelessly to catch this suspect. As the secretary for literary safety, I will make sure we have the protections needed for our most vulnerable back in place as soon as possible.

"In the meantime, we have removed much of the highest risk content from circulation as a precautionary measure. If you are a vulnerable person, please consider deactivating your reader until the Librarian is repaired. If you have friends or family who are vulnerable, please encourage them to do this and to seek additional counselling if necessary. It would be a tragedy if we let the actions of one terrorist succeed in spreading trauma.

"The Police Cybercrimes Unit has set up a hotline for any information about the suspect, Virginia Wright, and her associates. You can also find information and updates online with the hashtag #WheresWright. If you have any information, please get in touch."

Sera glanced down to check her phone as the journalists started yelling questions at the secretary. The hashtag was already trending, but just above it was another: #WheresRight. She looked it up and winced.

#WheresRight—the right to freedom of speech
#WheresRight—the right to freedom from arbitrary arrest

"Secretary Turnstin, what do you say to members of the public who have discovered they were subject to extensive censorship they were unaware of?" a journalist called out from nearby.

"Well, Deanna. I'd say that means we're doing our job right. They were protected from trauma in a way that didn't interfere with their life at all to the point that they didn't even notice. Next question."

Sera made a mental note to see if they could get Deanna Myers's network to reassign her elsewhere. She was becoming a problem.

"How many mental health admissions have there been since the Librarian went down?" a man called from the back of the room.

Sera glanced over and gave him the slightest of nods. She was glad she'd taken the time to prep him over coffee this morning. She'd been up since six a.m. trying to get the stats to say what they wanted.

"We saw a five percent rise immediately following the incident compared to the previous week. But I'm happy to say that's dropped by fifty percent since we took down the high-risk content," Bren answered, with a suitably concerned tone.

Sera checked her phone again and saw the graph she'd added to the press release popping up in the live-feeds. They'd be OK as long as the journalists didn't try and get their own data. Sera saw Deanna lean forward to start asking another question, and stepped away from the wall.

"That's all we have time for, sorry. Any further questions can be directed to the secretary's office," she said, opening the door for Bren to make his exit. They had this move well-practised.

Deanna's voice followed their departing backs— "Have you asked Ganelon Corporation to explain the discrepancies revealed in the leaked documents?"

Silence fell as the door clicked shut behind them. Not for the first time, Sera was grateful for the private exit.

"Perfect timing as always, Sera," Bren said.

"That's what you pay me for," she replied. "The hashtag is backfiring, by the way. Police didn't consult us on it. The human rights lobby is playing on the Virginia Wright/human right wording."

"Amateurs. Not much we can do now. When are we meeting Ganelon Corp?"

"Monday."

"Great. We need to come up with some messages on that discrepancy. Maybe do something symbolic."

Their footsteps echoed as they made their way back to the secretary's suite of offices. It was Saturday, so the usually busy corridors were deserted. None of their staff would be in and there were no meetings scheduled. Sera was walking a step behind Bren, and her eyes traced down his muscled back.

She held the door open for him when they reached their offices and her face flushed as he brushed against her on the way past. She was so distracted she almost didn't notice there was someone sitting on the couch in reception.

"Grace! What a lovely surprise! To what do I owe the pleasure?" Bren said.

He held her shoulders and kissed both her cheeks as she stood to greet him, his fingers trailing down her arms as they separated.

"I was at an event with Bob, but he was so busy I thought I'd just leave him to it and stretch my legs a bit."

Sera ignored Grace's suggestively raised eyebrow at those last words and nodded politely to the senator's wife.

"I'll be in my office if you need me," she said to Bren.

"Thank you, Serafina."

The cascade of Grace's flirtatious laughter followed after her as she left them to it.

Sera had been excited when she'd first moved into her office and realised it had its own door to Bren's. It was specially designed to let political aides eavesdrop on sensitive conversations they needed to hear.

They had taken full advantage of the discrete access to each other without the receptionist or the other staff being any the wiser, but she had quickly realised there were downsides.

Now, Sera's knuckles turned white where they gripped the armrests of her chair as the moaning noises from Bren's office reached a crescendo through the too-thin door. She gave up trying to return reporters' calls.

Silence finally fell and she heard Bren's office door open and close just as her phone rang. He sauntered into her office as she answered the call.

"Hello, Mrs Turnstin," she said.

Bren shook his head slightly as he perched himself on her desk.

"No. I'm sorry. He's been caught up in media questions from this afternoon. I'll have him call you as soon as he can," Sera said.

She leaned back in her chair and let her lips tighten the tiniest amount once she'd said goodbye to the secretary's wife and got off the phone.

Bren noticed and hung his head, playfully. "Am I in trouble?"

She stood up and went to pour herself a glass of water from the side table.

"Eve didn't sound angry," she replied.

His arms snaked around her from behind and he kissed her neck.

"I didn't mean with her."

Sera turned towards him, and the lingering smell of Grace's perfume wafted over her.

"At least it's a conservative senator. I'm sure I can work it out with Bob's office if we need to cover anything up. You smell like her. You need to change your shirt before you go home," she said.

Sera moved to pull away, but Bren kept one arm around her waist and started unbuttoning her shirt with the other hand.

Sera rolled her eyes. "I said your shirt, not mine. I don't know why you're chasing her so hard if she won't put out. I've got work to do."

"I'm sure your boss won't mind," Bren smirked.

"You need to call your wife."

Bren paused and then his hand reached up to cup her face and he kissed her gently. "So, I am in trouble then. You're the only one I can be honest with. You're the only one I would be lost without."

Sera wondered for the millionth time how she had ended up in this position and why she stayed there. It didn't stop her leaning forward to kiss him again, though.

When she got home that night, she spent long minutes staring at her face in the mirror. She reached up to touch her still swollen lips. She could hear her sister's voice in her head telling her to have some self-respect. That comment had been about compromising her political ideals to take a job with a conservative politician. She would hate to see the shame in her sister's eyes if she ever discovered what else was going on.

Sera turned off the light and went to bed, curling up in her cold sheets alone. Her sister had barely spoken to her since that argument and she missed her despite everything. Some words are hard to forgive, and apparently that included: "I want to keep you safe from the books that trigger your depression".

CHAPTER 2

Sera was always first to arrive at the office and Monday was no different. By the time Bren got in, she had already read and annotated three briefings from the Agency for Literary Safety, instructed the press staff on counteracting the dismal failure of the hashtag, and prepared speaking notes for each of the day's appointments.

She'd left the door between their offices open and she frowned as she listened to him joking with the receptionist. He only had ten minutes until his first meeting. She stood up as soon as she caught the flicker of movement from his office, and she was standing beside his desk by the time he sat down.

"Morning, Sera. How was the rest of your weekend?" he said.

"The Sunday news outlets stuck to the press release. Ms Myers doesn't seem to have gotten any traction with her angle, yet. You're meeting with Ganelon in five minutes. Your speaking points are here, including the details of the discrepancy between their recorded donations, and our official declaration."

Sera leaned forward to point to the relevant sections of the documents on his tablet and Bren caught her hand to kiss the inside of her wrist.

"I was asking about *your* weekend."

Sera pulled away and tapped the tablet again. "This was my weekend. It's a serious risk to your reappointment. Not only that, it could be the tipping point for public opinion on the Librarian. We've been lucky so far that the major news outlets have been running our public safety content. We can't assume that will continue."

Bren raised his hands in surrender. "I get it. Play hardball with Ganelon. I trust myself to your capable hands."

Sera let out an exasperated sigh at the innuendo, but couldn't help but smile. There was a reason Bren had been appointed as secretary of literary safety, and it certainly wasn't because of any expertise in censorship ethics, algorithms, or cybercrime. It was his damn charm. He could sell anything to anybody.

"Read the brief," she said, sternly.

"Yes, ma'am."

They left the Ganelon visitors waiting in reception just long enough to show who was in charge, and then Sera went to fetch them. She nodded in approval as she watched the two of them stand to greet her. The corporation had sent its board chair and its CEO. They were obviously taking this as seriously as she was.

The two corporate leaders were cut from the same cloth as Bren—all power postures, tailored suits, and charming smiles for even a lowly aide. But she was under no illusions that they would run rings around Bren if given the chance. He left the finer points of finances and technology to his flock of loyal staff.

"Mr Lesh. Ms Jamieson. The secretary will see you now," she said, exchanging firm handshakes with them.

"Lovely to see you again, Ms Olsen. I've been watching your deft management of the press over the last few weeks. Very impressive," CEO Marie Jamieson said.

"Thank you. It's a team effort. We are blessed with fantastic PR staff. It's certainly been a busy time," Sera said, as she led them into the office.

"But we all know you're driving the charge. And very capably," Marie said.

Sera shut the door as Bren stood up from behind his desk.

"I hope you're not trying to poach my staff, Marie!" he joked as he came to greet them.

"Their loyalty to you is renowned, Brenton. I don't know how you do it," Henry Lesh, the Ganelon board chair, chipped in.

Sera shot a glance at him as she made her way to a seat off to the side of Bren's desk. Was it her imagination or had there been the slightest tone to that remark? An implication that he knew exactly how Bren kept her particular loyalty.

They'd run this kind of good-cop/bad-cop routine in the past. Henry playing hardball and Marie smoothing things over. This was going to be an interesting meeting. Bren just laughed and gestured to them to take their seats.

Once everyone was seated, Bren leaned forward on his desk and steepled his hands.

"So, we have a problem. I love the work Ganelon has done for us developing the Librarian algorithm, and obviously we both want to see our partnership continue, but I need to show I'm doing something about these leaked documents and the complaints coming through from the public. You left a vulnerability in the system that allowed the freedom lobby to hack it and remove all the restrictions. You've put our citizens at risk and meanwhile I'm fielding dozens of calls a day from the general public asking why their readers have so many restrictions they knew nothing about. What are you going to do about it and why isn't it done already?" Bren said.

Henry leaned forward in his chair like it was his own office he was sitting in, the smile gone from his face. "Firstly, the only vulnerability was the ineptitude of your police officers and your agency's rushed implementation of the new functions. Secondly, our contract clearly stipulates that responsibility for decisions on what is restricted lies with your agency, not with Ganelon. Any issues or liability associated with that are *your* responsibility, not ours."

Bren stared at Henry with the beginnings of a frown and Sera jumped in. "That is accurate. Except where the fault lies with your coding and not our instruction, which has yet to be established. And it seems highly unlikely that the lobby could have identified this particular vulnerability without inside information on the system; inside information that only your staff would have access to."

Marie held her hands up in a placating gesture— "Establishing who was responsible for the past isn't going to solve the problems we're facing right now in the present. We all agree we want the partnership to continue. Let's start from there."

Sera opened her mouth to continue arguing the point. Establishing who was responsible would tell them who needed to pay to fix it, or who needed to fall on their sword to placate the media. But before she could start talking, Bren held a hand up to stop her.

"We can come back to the question of responsibility later. What do you suggest? People are calling for a public inquiry," Bren said.

"There's no need to panic just yet. These things often blow over. Give it a few more weeks. We can try some things on our side to edge opinion along a bit," Marie said.

Bren was nodding, but Sera's eyes had narrowed in suspicion. "What kind of things?" she asked.

"All totally above board, of course. We'll just shift the new releases around a bit. Get our content generators putting out some stories. Make sure people's readers are pointing them at something reassuring about the protective State. We've got some crime and romance stories using the new police search functions that should do the job," Marie said.

"And what about the press? What about Deanna Myers?" Sera asked.

"A little tweak to our advertising targeting and budgets and the big players will all stay in line. Especially if you keep feeding them stories they can run with a better angle."

Sera caught Bren's eye and shook her head. It wasn't going to be enough. The protestors weren't children to be swayed by stories. Hoping people would forget and move along to the next crisis was not a strategy. Ganelon was just hoping to avoid being hauled before an inquiry to explain itself. An inquiry that could show the secretary took people's concerns seriously and was doing his job.

"So, I'm supposed to just watch my approval ratings plummet while you profit from a bunch of stories we let you push up the algorithm?" Bren said.

Sera watched the two visitors exchange a look, and Henry took over speaking.

"As a gesture of good faith, we could offer you one of our staff as liaison in your office. They could give you visibility of the kinds of content we'd be putting through. We could tailor the stories for your particular needs. There's an election coming up before your reappointment. It would be a shame to miss the opportunity to get some good old-fashioned values coming through."

Sera watched Bren's eyes light up at the political opportunities opening up before him. The chance to undermine his opponents in the public's subconscious. She swore silently to herself. They had targeted his weakness perfectly.

"Bren, could I have a word in private?" she said.

"Not now, Sera."

"I have to advise against—"

Bren cut her off— "I said not now, Sera."

Henry was watching her reaction. Her eyes narrowed as she saw the corner of his mouth twitch. He knew he'd won. His eyes stayed on hers as he continued speaking.

"We have a romance series we could model you into as well, Brenton. See if we can't bump up your polling with the ladies. Subtly, of course. You wouldn't want people to notice."

Sera's teeth hurt from gritting them so hard as she glared at Henry. Bren was already busy talking options. Henry's veiled threat had gone right over his head. How had he found out about them? He must have someone in the office already, or it was bugged. Either that or he'd hacked their phone messages. Her cheeks flushed red at the thought and she broke eye contact with Henry, pretending to record notes while she got herself back under control.

"Are you getting all this down, Sera? You'll need to find a desk for their liaison and brief them on my ideas. When can they start?" Bren asked, turning back to Henry.

"We can have someone here tomorrow."

"Private companies are not permitted to have staff in the office. It's a conflict of interest," Sera said in a clipped voice.

Henry smiled at her. "I'm sure a lady of your talents can work something out," he said.

"Sera's amazing. She'll make it happen," Bren agreed.

Sera hung back as Bren shook hands in farewell. Her breakfast was churning in her stomach. What had just happened? Bren shut the door behind them and turned back to her.

"What's wrong? That was a great outcome for everyone," he said.

"That was bribery. Or blackmail, depending on how you look at it," she snapped.

"Stop being so dramatic. It was a business deal."

"You're not in business. You're in public service. And if this deal goes south, it could destroy you and all the good the Librarian has done!"

Bren came over to her and pulled her stiff body into his arms. "But it won't, because I have you looking out for me."

"I can only look out for you if you listen to my advice. This is wrong. It's not ethical," she said, pushing him away.

He held tight to her shoulders, refusing to move away. "This is what we need to do to keep the Librarian going, to keep protecting people. If our opponents see public opinion is against us, they'll campaign on shutting it down. If we can use this to keep the public on side, then it doesn't even matter if I get reappointed. Both sides will keep the Librarian in place. Your sister will stay safe."

Bren had manipulated her just as carefully as Henry had manipulated him. He knew why she was here. He even knew she didn't agree with most of his politics. Getting the Librarian algorithm in place to protect people had always been enough to keep her there. That and the damn sex. Bren could keep anyone loyal.

Sera sighed and felt the tension leave her muscles as her shoulders slumped in defeat. There was nothing to do even if she'd wanted to. She was sure Henry's threat was very real and he probably already had a successor lined up if Bren didn't play nicely. He had connections everywhere. She wouldn't gain anything from fighting him and becoming the front-page sex scandal that brought Bren down.

"Your next appointment will be waiting," she said.

Bren placed a finger under her chin and tilted her head up to kiss her.

"Don't look so despondent. We're doing good things here. It will all work out. You'll see."

CHAPTER 3

Sera didn't believe in relying on things to work out. She believed in planning and contingencies, which is why the first thing she did when she was back in her office was to find someone to look into Ganelon.

She knew they were questionable already, but all the dirt she had on them was just as bad for the secretary's office as it was for Ganelon. What she needed was something personal; something like what they had on her. That wasn't the kind of thing she could ask the staff to look into. This needed a different kind of digging.

Her eyes trailed down the search results for private investigators on her screen. A name caught her attention, jogging a memory: Cameron Palmer. Why did she know that name?

She searched her records and found a hit. Cameron Palmer: 'retired' from the cyber-crimes division of the police after the incident where his partner Detective Virginia Wright had hacked the police system to spread the virus that took out the Librarian restrictions across 80 percent of readers within the space of hours.

Palmer would be perfect. She suspected he had sympathies with the freedom lobby or he wouldn't have lost his job. He'd be personally motivated to find the dirt on Ganelon, and if she was a client he would be forced to keep it confidential once he found it.

She dialled his number, fidgeting as the phone rang. She needed to set the investigation up before the Ganelon 'liaison' started the next day. She was going to have to call the liaison her intern and sacrifice half her office to his desk. She wouldn't be able to handle anything confidential there from tomorrow, like whatever Palmer managed to dig up. What a mess.

"Hello, Mr Palmer?"—she said when he answered— "My name's Serafina. I have an investigation I need help with. It must be treated with the utmost discretion. Can you help?"

"What are the details?" Cameron said.

"It would be better to speak in person. Three p.m. at the coffee place by the cenotaph?"

"Ah, sure. I can do that."

"Perfect. See you then."

Sera spent the rest of the morning organising furniture and the hundred admin details that came with letting someone whose name you didn't even know, and whose company affiliation you were hiding, work in a highly secure building with one day's notice. It wasn't like she'd had anything else to do.

Bren wandered in through their shared door at lunchtime and stood behind her rubbing her shoulders as she typed out another email. His hand snuck further down her front as she ignored him. She could feel his breath on her neck as he kissed her before looking across at the new desk and chair taking up all the spare floor space.

"He's going to be sitting in here? How are we going to…"

"You should have thought of that before you told them he could come," Sera said, pushing his hand away so she could concentrate on what she was doing.

Bren spun her chair around to face him and pulled her to her feet.

"I thought we'd been over this. We agreed it was the right thing to do," he said.

Sera shrugged. "It's happening, right or not. And he can't be with the rest of the staff. He's a security risk. Not to mention that if they get wind of where he's from, we can't guarantee they won't whistle-blow. He has to be in here. I'm going to need to use your office for any confidential calls, and you're going to have to watch your volume while he's around. Don't give them any more ammunition to blackmail you with."

"They're not going to blackmail me. We're partners. We need each other."

"Henry insinuated he knows about us. He was threatening me," Sera said, slowing her words down as if he was being particularly thick, which he was.

"You're reading too much into it," Bren said, wrapping his arms around her again and trying to distract her with another kiss.

Sera had lost patience with the discussion. Bren was naïve if he thought everyone was going to come out of this smelling of roses.

"It's my job to read into things. Speaking of which, you have six briefings you should be reading," she said, pushing him away and sitting back down to return to her work.

She could see she'd pissed him off. His chiselled jaw was even sharper as he clenched it, angry at her rejection.

"Just remember who works for who here, Serafina." His voice had chilled.

He stalked away from her desk and then turned back at the door to his office. "Oh, and message Grace for me. Tell her I'm free at three for a coffee in my office if she wants to stretch her legs."

"You have a meeting with the mental health charity at three," Sera said, careful to keep her voice even.

"Reschedule."

She waited until the door shut with a bang before swearing under her breath.

Private investigator, Cameron Palmer, was waiting outside the coffee shop by the time Sera arrived that afternoon. She looked him up and down as she approached. She'd imagined someone older. There was no way this thirty-something man with his smart-casual collared shirt and jeans had 'retired'. The scar on his left temple where his partner had knocked him out when she hacked the system was still red.

"Mr Palmer. Thank you for meeting me," Sera said, reaching out to shake his hand.

"My pleasure, Ms Olsen."

Sera followed him into the shop, pleased he'd identified her. She'd wondered how long it would take him to figure out who she was. It had been a test of sorts.

They made polite small-talk until their coffees arrived, and then Palmer took a sip from his steaming cup and cut to the chase.

"So, Ms Olsen. Are you employing me personally or on behalf of your employer?"

"A little bit of both. He's paying the bill."

Palmer raised an eyebrow. "I see."

Sera glanced around to check no one was close enough to hear and then leaned forward so she could speak more quietly. "I need you to dig up anything you can on Henry Lesh and Marie Jamieson. If it has to do with the company, fine. If it's about them personally, all the better."

Palmer leaned back in his chair for a moment and looked thoughtful. "Leverage?"

"Insurance."

"I would've thought you'd be best buddies. Why investigate now?" Palmer asked.

Sera searched his face for what was behind the question. If he was any good at his job, he'd figure it out pretty quickly anyway.

"Brenton and I have a very… close relationship. Henry seems to have noticed and he thought he'd mention it to me."

"Ah, I see. Do many people notice?" Palmer asked delicately.

"No. No one. How long do you need?"

"Their security will be tight. I should have some leads within a week or two, and we can check in on how you want to proceed. I can email you my hourly rate and contract."

"Phone and cash only. Here's a deposit," Sera said, slipping an envelope to him under the table.

Palmer thumbed through the contents and then looked up at her and nodded. "This will cover the first two weeks."

"Call me when you have something. I'll need you to come check the offices for bugs this weekend as well."

She drained her coffee and left.

Sera got into the office early the next morning. Ganelon's liaison showed up at seven a.m. sharp, an hour before the receptionist or anyone else would arrive.

She went down to the entrance to let him through security. He was putting a collection of five e-readers back into his bag after the security scans as she arrived.

He had a mop of ginger hair and pale skin that showed the dark circles under his eyes, but when he looked up at her she could see he was alert and calculating.

"Serafina? I'm your new intern, Matty Greene," he said, holding out his hand.

"Welcome, Matty. Come this way."

She was the perfect host as they made their way through the corridors, pointing out the corridor to the senators' wing and the staff cafeteria. She waved to other early-starters as they passed, introducing Matty.

As soon as they were through into the secretary's suite of offices, she turned to him.

"Let me be absolutely clear. Your presence here will be tightly monitored. You are not to engage with any of the other staff. You will not be permitted to read any documents that are not already available to the public. We can cancel your access at any time, for any reason. If asked, your job is filing my emails and contacting donors. Your desk is in my office, so I can keep an eye on you," she said.

Matty ignored her sharp tone and smiled. "If your boss is happy, my boss is happy. I won't cause any problems if you don't."

Sera frowned. What was that supposed to mean?

Matty settled himself at his new desk and busied himself with his various readers. Sera tried to focus on her own job, but she kept catching herself frowning at the back of his head. She was grateful for the distraction when Bren walked in the door an hour later.

"Good Morning, Serafina. Ah! Our new liaison has arrived!" Bren said, walking over to greet Matty.

"Our new *intern*," Sera corrected, standing up to shut the door to reception before anyone overheard them.

"Matty Greene. It's an honour to meet you, sir." Matty held out his hand and Bren shook it enthusiastically.

"Is that really necessary?" Bren said, gesturing towards the door.

Sera held his gaze, pointedly. "I messaged you the relevant protocol yesterday," she said.

"I didn't have time to read that whole thing. You should have just put it in the message."

Sera's eyes flicked to Matty, who was watching with a politely bland expression on his face but she could see he was following closely.

"Some things are best left unwritten, *sir*. A liaison would require a number of approvals, a conflict of interest management plan, and the potential for public scrutiny."

Bren looked like he was going to reignite their argument from the day before, but then he smiled and clapped her shoulder, instead.

"She's always looking out for me, this one," he said to Matty. "Now, what about these stories Henry was talking about?"

"I've got five options for you to review already, sir," Matty said.

Sera returned to her desk and left them to it. The less she had to do with this plan, the better. Bren looked up from Matty's screen as she was lowering herself back into her chair.

"Oh, Sera? I wanted to send some poetry to my appointment from yesterday afternoon. Something sophisticated, but with the right kind of… mood. Could you find something?" he said.

He didn't even wait for her response before returning to his reading. Matty glanced over at her and the corner of his mouth twitched. She wished she could knock the smug look off his face. How long was she going to have to put up with this?

"Of course, sir. I'll send you something shortly," she said.

Sera knew Bren didn't read anything sophisticated, and neither did Grace. She could send anything and they wouldn't have a clue, which meant she could safely indulge her annoyance.

She skimmed through Shakespeare's *Venus and Adonis* for something with appropriate innuendo. Bren didn't need to know he was the Venus in their story, or how tragic the ending was.

She copied a stanza and sent it through to him. He would send it directly from his reader to Grace's. Knowing him, he would probably wait for the next time they were at an event together. He liked to live dangerously and he would want to watch her face while she read it next to her husband.

The tender spring upon thy tempting lip
Shows thee unripe yet mayst thou well be tasted:
Make use of time, let not advantage slip;
Beauty within itself should not be wasted:

COMPACT OF FIRE

Fair flowers that are not gathered in their prime
Rot and consume themselves in little time...

...Love is a spirit all compact of fire...

CHAPTER 4

The week passed in a flurry of public relations management. Even with the media on side, people kept discovering more stories that had been censored from their readers. The hashtag #WheresRight just wouldn't die.

No matter how much they tried to focus attention on the hunt for the suspect, they couldn't shift the slowly growing group of people that saw Ms Wright as some sort of modern-day Robin Hood. Bren's charm offensive was only getting them so far.

Sera's phone buzzed on the desk and she took a break from crafting the latest press release to check it. She stretched her back as she picked up her phone.

Dinner's at six. Don't be late.

She couldn't hold back her sigh. The last thing she wanted after this week was another awkward family meal.

I'll do my best, Ma, she replied.

Matty glanced up at the noise in their otherwise silent office.

"Everything OK?" he asked.

Sera was getting used to having him around, which is just as well because it was Saturday and he'd still come into the office. She was going to have to make sure he wasn't around when Palmer showed up tonight.

Matty was actually alright company when he wasn't trying to play power games. She opened her mouth to respond, but before she could speak a woman's breathless giggle drifted through the walls from Bren's office. Both of their eyes flicked to the internal door.

Sera forced her attention back to Matty. "Yeah, everything's fine. Just family stuff," she said.

Matty tilted his head to the side and watched her. "Why do you let him get away with that?" he asked, gesturing towards the door.

"It's not my place to tell him how to live his life. I'm not his wife," she said.

"But, you're something," Matty said.

Sera could feel his eyes searching her face. Was he just curious? Or was he looking for a weakness to exploit? Probably both. She shrugged noncommittally in answer to his question.

"Plus, he's leaving himself exposed. It makes your job that much harder. Why stick around?" he pressed.

He was definitely sniffing for a weakness.

"Because I believe in what he's doing. In the Librarian program. And he's good at what he does. He wins people over and that's what we need most to succeed," Sera said.

Matty's eyebrows raised in surprise. "Huh. I hadn't picked you for an idealist."

A stiff smile crept across her face as she watched him process the information. He'd been looking for a jealous lover and found something else. She wondered what he would report back to his bosses. She knew she'd have to tread even more carefully now. They had obviously thought they could use her supposed jealousy to manipulate her. They'd be looking for another weakness now. She should have let him keep his false assumptions. She went back to her work without saying anything more.

Bren came in ten minutes later to perch on her desk next to her chair, his legs brushing against hers. His tie was hanging loose and too many of his shirt buttons were undone. Sera's mouth tightened. He was getting careless, and he was too trusting of Matty.

"That poetry was perfect, Sera. Really did the trick," Bren said.

"My pleasure," Sera said, drily, just so she could watch Matty struggle to keep his smirk hidden. There had to be some advantages to having a voyeur in her office.

Bren looked concerned and reached out to stroke a finger across her hand on the keyboard, which was barely out of sight from Matty behind her screen.

"Let's do dinner tonight. I feel like I haven't seen you in ages," he said, softly.

"I can't. I'm going to my mother's."

Bren frowned. "Come talk me through those briefings then." He pushed himself up from the desk.

"I've got some things I need to finish up here," she said, focusing on her screen.

Bren spun her chair around to face him. "They can wait," he said. Then he looked over at Matty— "Thanks for your help, Matty. You can go home. We'll see you on Monday."

Matty smiled. "You're very welcome. You know, poetry can be a bit dated. If you wanted something a bit more modern next time, I'm happy to help. Maybe something a bit more personal, too."

"That's not necessary," Sera said, firmly.

"But much appreciated. Fantastic idea. Send something through," Bren said.

"I'll get right on it," Matty said, turning back to his computer.

"Right, let's sort those briefings out," Bren said, pulling Sera to her feet, apparently already forgetting he'd asked Matty to leave.

She tried to pull her hand away as he led her to his office, but he kept hold of it. So much for keeping up at least a pretence of a professional relationship. Bren shut the door behind them and pushed her up against it, pressing his lips to hers.

She pushed him away and hissed "Stop it. He's right there. I have to work with him every day, damn it!"

"He doesn't care," Bren said, leaning in to kiss her neck.

"So, you admit he knows, then? I care," she said, pushing him away again.

"Is this about Grace? It's not like you to be jealous."

He still had his body pushed up against hers, one of his hands behind her neck ready to pull her in again.

"I'm not jealous. But if she's leaving you... unsatisfied, that's not my problem."

She felt Bren's hand tighten on her neck, his thumb pressing too hard on her throat. Her eyes widened and she pushed him away harder.

"I said stop it. You're hurting me."

The moment of anger left Bren's face and his grip loosened. He reached up to stroke her cheek.

"I'm sorry, sweetheart. You're right. Matty's stories will help I'm sure and then things can go back to normal."

Sera looked away and focused her attention on the antique lamp resting on his desk, hoping he would take the hint and move away. This wasn't like him; it wasn't like them. She'd thought Grace was just another of his trophies to chase, but she was starting to wonder if Grace wasn't the one playing the game.

"You're leaving yourself open to blackmail from Ganelon and from Grace," she said.

"You always see the worst in people. We're all on the same side," he said with a frown, finally moving away.

Sera reached up to touch the place his hands had squeezed her throat. He had lost control, but if she let it fall apart now he would tear the whole Librarian system down with him when he went. All her work and all her sacrifice—of family and self-respect— would be for nothing.

She walked up behind him and wrapped her arms around him, reaching her hand up to pull his head back towards her. Maybe she could distract him from Grace before things got too bad. Before he fell even further into Matty's trap. Her eyes stayed trained on the antique lamp again as she lay back on the desk.

She was only twenty minutes late for dinner. Her mother didn't say anything, just stood to the side to let her into the apartment. Her sister looked up from the table where all the food sat untouched and cooling.

"Nice of you to join us," she said, not bothering to wait for Sera to sit down before reaching out to spoon lukewarm mashed potato onto her plate.

"That's enough, Riley!" Sera's ma said.

"What? I said it was nice."

Sera sighed and pulled out a chair while her mum went to fetch some water from the kitchen.

"Your love-bite's showing over your collar. How is the good secretary these days?" Riley whispered.

Sera blushed and readjusted her shirt, ignoring the question as their ma returned to the table. She hadn't realised Riley had guessed what was going on. So much for no one knowing.

They all busied themselves serving and for a moment it was like it used to be when they were kids. The clink of cutlery, the smell of slightly over-cooked meat, the dishes placed just so to cover the holes in the tablecloth their mother couldn't bear to throw away. Sera took a bite of her meal and was still chewing the tough mouthful when her mother spoke up.

"So, what are you both up to? I haven't seen you in weeks."

Riley looked over at Sera and held her eyes with her own as she replied. "I'm helping organise the big protest march next week. We've got some great speakers coming. Want to hear the chants?"

Their mother's eyes flicked between her two daughters. "That's nice, dear. Maybe later. What about you, Sera? What are you doing with your free time? Are you still practising your cello?" Her sentences came too fast, tumbling over each other as she tried to deflect the conversation and avoid the fight she knew was brewing.

"Why are you so set against the Librarian, Ri? You of all people should know why it's needed," Sera said, restarting the argument that had played out dozens of times before. It was like picking at a scab, simultaneously satisfying and scarring.

"Me, of all people? Because I'm 'traumatised'? Because I need to be 'protected' like I'm some kind of child?" Riley sneered.

"Because it can help you stay safe!"

Sera reached out and shoved Riley's sleeve up before she had time to jerk away, revealing the white raised lines of past scars marching up her wrist like the rungs of a ladder. There was a single fresh cut at the top. Sera hadn't expected that. Hadn't realised her sister was struggling again. She yanked her hand back like she'd been burned.

The clash of her mother's fork dropping onto a plate snapped her out of her shock.

"Stop it! Both of you!" her ma cried.

The two grown women stared down at their plates like they were nine and ten years old again.

"Riley. Are you OK?"

"She's got access to all those damn masochistic writers again," Sera snapped.

"I didn't ask you!" Her mother snapped back even louder.

Sera glared at them both. Why did they always make her feel like the bad guy?

Riley had pushed her sleeve back down and sat playing with the hem of her cuff.

"I'm fine," she muttered.

Sera watched her sister with a pained expression. Another thing to worry about. As if she didn't have enough going on. She wasn't worried Riley would do anything drastic. That wasn't what it was about. This was how it always started, though. First came the cuts, then came the latest addiction—alcohol, gambling, or whatever—until they had to stage an intervention. It was why she'd never gone into politics herself. Too much family baggage. She took a breath to calm down. Maybe they could nip it in the bud this time.

"Why don't you give us your reader? Just until the system's working again," Sera said softly, reaching out to try and hold Riley's hand.

"It's got nothing to do with the damn reader!" Riley shouted, her chair screeching across the floor as she shoved herself to her feet.

Sera fought to stay calm while her mother held a hand to her temples. Surely, she could make her sister see reason.

"That cut is recent. You were doing fine until the restrictions were hacked. You don't have to read that stuff. You don't have to hate yourself."

Sera's voice cracked on the last sentence, pleading. She wasn't sure if she was speaking to her sister or herself.

Her sister's response was so low she almost couldn't make it out. "I don't hate myself. I've just realised how much you hate me. How much you're willing to take from me with your precious Librarian."

Sera was so shocked she couldn't even run after Riley as she stormed from the apartment. She looked over at her mother, still leaning on the table with her face buried in her hands.

"I don't hate her. I'm just trying to keep her safe," she whispered.

Her mother looked up with red-rimmed eyes. "A well-meaning mistake is still a mistake. I can't do this right now. All I wanted was a nice dinner with my daughters. I'm going to bed."

Sera stood up and watched her ma shuffle away like she had aged twenty years since she walked in the door. She looked so frail.

"Are you OK, Ma?"

Her mother raised a hand in farewell without turning around and opened the door to her bedroom. Sera stood by the table wondering how things had gone even worse than she'd expected. She'd never realised her ma agreed with her sister about the Librarian. How long had she been pretending to support her?

Her phone vibrated in her pocket and she pulled it out with numb fingers. It was a message from Palmer.

Are we still on for 9pm?

She'd almost forgotten he was coming to sweep the office for bugs.

Yes. See you soon, she replied.

She cleared the dishes away and put the food in the fridge before she left. She looked around one last time before she turned the lights off. She noticed the board game her ma had optimistically left on the coffee table in the hopes they could have made it through an entire evening together.

She opened the lid and stared at the familiar game pieces. It had been years since they'd given up on the weekly family games night. Her sister had always played the wizard to her alchemist. She picked up her sister's piece, a mystic green flame, and put in her pocket, gripping it tight. She could feel the tips of the flame sharp against her fingers as she walked out the door.

CHAPTER 5

The shadows cast by the streetlights left Sera searching the darkness for imagined threats as she made her way back to the Government complex that housed the secretary's offices.

She usually loved this time of night, when the relentless traffic noise reduced to a whisper and the breeze was freed from carrying daytime's scents of road-side food vendors and exhaust. But her sister had set her on edge, and she realised she was dreading what Palmer might uncover.

She'd arranged to meet him by a side door where there was no security. With any luck, no one would look back at the footage and realise he'd been there. He was already waiting just outside of the circle of light from the entrance when she arrived, his dark grey trench coat melding with the shadowy grey stone of the wall behind him.

"Ms Olsen," he said, nodding in greeting.

"Mr Palmer."

Sera swiped her access card and let them both inside, her heart skipping a beat as the motion-sensors made the hallway lights flick on. Why was she so jumpy? The two of them strode silently through the building until they reached the offices. Everything was dark. She'd been the last to leave that evening, but a small part of her had worried that Matty might come back.

She gestured to her office and Bren's next to it. "It's just those two we need to check. Everywhere else is not so... sensitive," she said.

"Got it," said Palmer.

She followed him into the office and watched as put his bag down and started searching every fixture and shelf, his fingers feeling for anything his eyes might miss.

"Aren't you going to use a sensor or something?" she asked.

"I'll do that next. You never know when they might come up with some new tech that a sensor won't pick up, though."

Sera left him to it. No point standing around doing nothing when she could be working. As she sat down at her desk, she felt the game piece in her pocket stab her leg. She took it out and placed it underneath her screen. A visual reminder that it could all go up in flames at any moment.

She logged onto her computer and looked up the protest march her sister had talked about. It was scheduled for Tuesday lunchtime and it already had ten thousand followers. She sighed and started writing up a briefing on it. She was still profiling the organisers when Palmer finished sweeping her office.

"I haven't found anything. Can I check your phone and reader?" he said.

Sera unlocked them and pushed them across her desk to him, watching as he ran diagnostics looking for anything that didn't belong.

"Well?" she asked, finally.

He looked up and shrugged. "There's nothing here. My best guess is they've tapped Secretary Turnstin's phone or they found out in some other way. Assuming you weren't communicating by reader. They would almost certainly be able to access reader communications."

Sera winced. Not finding the bug wasn't great news, but it could be worse. "It would have to be his personal phone. The work ones are too secure. How do we fix it?"

"I'd suggest arranging an accident for the phone and making sure you control the replacement. But if he doesn't look after it better, it will just happen again."

"And the damage has already been done. Did you find anything else this week?" Sera asked.

"The official records on Mr Lesh and Ms Jamieson are so vanilla that they must have been doctored. The company records are a maze of shell-companies and anonymous trusts. I've yet to find anything you would call a smoking gun. There are rumours of staff who have disappeared. Several politicians and competitors who have spoken against them have found themselves disgraced. But there is no proof anywhere. Nothing to tie it back to them. I did find one surprising investment—a domestic airport just out of town that operates cargo planes. I can't think what Ganelon would need it for, but there's nothing to suggest it's doing anything illegal."

Sera rubbed her aching temples. Why had she never heard about these disappearances before?

"So, we've got nothing? Would your friend Ms Wright know anything?"

Palmer's voice chilled. "I am not in contact with Ms Wright. And if that's what this was really about, you can find someone else to do your investigating."

Sera searched his face for any sign he was lying, but he just looked angry.

"I'm not asking for her location. I just thought she might have some information that would be useful."

Palmer pulled the zipper on his bag closed so hard it almost snapped off. "We're done here."

Sera sighed. How had this week fallen apart so quickly?

"I'll show you out," she said.

Sera spent Sunday in the office, preparing for what she knew would be a nightmare week. By the time Monday rolled around, she'd only been home to sleep and change her clothes.

She ignored Matty when he arrived at the office, only looking up from her computer when Bren walked in the door.

"Morning, team. How's that story coming, Matty?" he asked.

Sera cut across the conversation before Matty could reply.

"The protest march on Tuesday has twenty-six thousand followers now. You're meeting with the police chief at ten to discuss crowd management. You need to get something from him on the Wright issue while he's here. We need something to announce. Something to distract people."

"There's no need to panic. They'll be lucky if a tenth of those people show up," Matty said.

Sera glared across the room at him and opened her mouth to respond, but Bren came and placed a hand on her shoulder before she could start.

"We can sort it all out with the police chief later. Matty's right, no need to panic. Now, have you got that story?" Bren asked.

"Yes, Sir. I've made the edits you suggested. It's ready to go," Matty said.

"Excellent. Can you load it and send it through to Grace for me?"

Bren held his reader out to Matty, but Sera intercepted it.

"I should do that for you," she said, pointedly.

Bren tilted her chin up with a finger to look at him. "Relax," he said, but he did pass her the reader, instead.

"Party polling has dropped five percent since the protest took off. They'll be expecting an explanation if you can't pull it back."

Bren frowned as his hand dropped away. "Has someone been in touch?"

"Not yet. You need to show strong action here. Take control and show people you're listening. Either we catch Wright this week or we need to launch a commission into the breach."

Matty stood up and approached the other side of the desk, leaning forward. "The last thing we need is a commission."

"The last thing *you* need is a commission,"—Sera corrected— "We need it to buy some breathing space.

47

We can keep the scope tight, put in someone we trust as Chair."

Bren was listening now, nodding along thoughtfully. "We can get the victim support groups to give evidence. Keep the narrative in line with our messaging."

"I'll need to call my boss," Matty said.

"It's got nothing to do with your boss. The secretary doesn't need your permission," Sera snapped back.

Matty pressed the screen on the reader he was still holding and Sera felt Bren's reader vibrate in her hand.

"Of course. It would be a shame if a commission came across anything inappropriate, though," Matty said.

Sera felt Bren stiffen beside her and she almost rolled her eyes. How damn naïve could he be? Had he been desperate enough to give Ganelon even more leverage? She glanced down at the reader and saw the cover artwork of the story Matty had just sent through for Grace. It involved a riding crop and restraints and left nothing to the imagination.

"I'm sure we can come to a solution that will work for everyone," she said through gritted teeth.

She managed not to let rip at Bren until they were safely ensconced in his office prepping for the meeting with the police chief later that morning. She'd glanced over the first chapter of the story by then and it was enough to make her ill. She hadn't realised how comparatively healthy their relationship was until that moment.

"What the hell, Bren? They've got you over a barrel. Have you lost your mind? You cannot send that to Grace."

Bren snatched the reader back off her and put it in a drawer. "She already got the first one on the weekend. This is the sequel," he muttered.

"You'll be lucky if she doesn't report you." Her voice shook as she tried to get control back. He was going to ruin everything.

Bren stroked a finger down her face. "Don't worry about that. We met up on Sunday. She was very... appreciative."

Sera felt bile rising up in her throat and pushed his hand away.

"Whatever. Keep me out of it. The less I know the better. You need to read that briefing before the chief arrives."

He pulled her closer. "Don't be like that. I need you to look after me, to keep me in line."

Sera just about gagged at the suggestive tone in his voice. He had definitely changed. She wondered how much of that change had come from him and how much from Matty's stories and Grace. They'd taken his addiction and twisted it into something else.

"I'm not… That's not…" she said.

Bren laughed low in his throat and pushed her onto the desk, but they were interrupted by the phone ringing. Sera grabbed for it and answered before he could get any more ideas.

"Ms Olsen, the police chief has arrived," the receptionist said down the line.

"Thank you, Beth. I'll come to collect him," she said.

Bren was still blocking her from getting off the desk with his body. That familiar smile that had always seemed too charming was losing its sheen. And then her heart sank as her whirling thoughts connected the dots of his behaviour—the way he'd shut her down when she tried to play hardball with Ganelon, the way he'd said they wouldn't blackmail him because they were partners, the impossible speed at which their 'liaison' had been secured. And even earlier than all that, the stalled negotiations with the Corporation when the latest literary safety laws were being debated that had inexplicably resolved overnight.

"You have an arrangement with them already. It was you who told them about us," she whispered.

Bren's grin widened. "They needed reassurance that you wouldn't whistle blow. I told Matty you'd catch on. He thought it would take longer. Ganelon won't let me get thrown out. We just need to keep things ticking over. You can relax about that, OK? I still need you to help me keep them in line, though."

"You can't just let them take control. This is people's lives we're talking about," Sera pleaded.

"This is a win-win if you let it be. Don't make it get ugly. You would hardly come out of it smelling of roses," Bren said.

Sera pushed him away and he resisted for a moment before backing off. She straightened her shirt and went to fetch their guest. Her brain couldn't function through the numb fog that had descended on her. How long had he been a puppet for Ganelon?

She barely heard the chief as he confirmed they still had no leads on Virginia Wright's location. A distant part of her wondered if Ganelon had something on the police chief, too. But of course, they would. She was still staring vacantly towards the back of the room when Bren returned from showing him out. He pulled her to her feet and kissed her, looking concerned.

"Why don't you take the afternoon off? Get your head together. I'm sure Matty can cover things."

She shook her head, trying to shake away the paralyzing spiral of thoughts at the same time. She needed time to think. She couldn't arouse their suspicion until she'd figured out what she was going to do.

"No. I'm fine. It's win-win like you said." She forced herself to smile and kiss him back.

His arms were wrapping around her waist when Matty knocked on the door between their offices. Bren exhaled in annoyance and reached out to pull it open without even bothering to let her go.

Sera watched as Matty purposefully avoided looking at Bren's hand resting on her hip. He spoke as if nothing had changed, his voice eminently professional.

"Mr Lesh agrees that a tightly-controlled commission is the best way to go. He complimented Ms Olsen on her foresight," he said.

"I told you. She's a genius at this kind of thing," Bren said, pulling her closer to kiss her cheek.

Sera smiled robotically and pulled away from his embrace so they were no longer touching.

"I have a lot to do if you want to announce that tomorrow," she said.

"Happy to help in any way I can," Matty said.

"Perfect. I will leave it with the two of you," Bren said.

Sera nodded and moved towards her office, careful to keep to a walk instead of running away from him like every nerve in her body was telling her to do. As she shut the door behind her, she saw Bren reaching into his desk drawer to get his reader out and send the next story to Grace. She couldn't help but shake her head in despair.

When she turned around, Matty was standing by her desk watching her closely.

"Do we have a problem?" he asked.

Sera stared at him blankly for a moment. Was it a problem that she was helping enable corporate corruption to take hold in government? Was it a problem that she was helping use taxpayer dollars to seduce another man's wife for her lover who was also married and her boss? "Problem" was far too tame a word. But she could hear Palmer's voice from the other night: *rumours of staff who have disappeared.* Sometimes honesty was the best way to lie.

"I know when I'm backed into a corner with nowhere to run. Shall we sort out this commission?" she said.

○

CHAPTER 6

Matty wasn't stupid enough to arouse suspicion by coming to the press conference the next day, so Sera walked alone with Bren down the corridors just like they always had. She was careful to avoid brushing up against him as they walked. She didn't trust his increasing lack of control.

"Appointing Bob as chair of this commission was a stroke of brilliance. Having Matty in the office to help you is really paying off," Bren said.

Sera made a noncommittal sound. She'd argued vehemently with Matty against appointing Grace's husband. It would be obvious to anyone who knew politics that something was going on. Bob wasn't a competent enough senator to head something this sensitive. She wondered if Bren realised Matty's plan was to use his affair with Grace against Bob if he made trouble, or if Bren just thought it was an excuse to see her more often. She'd tried to explain it to him, but he didn't want to hear it.

"How do I look?" he said, turning to her as they reached the side entrance to the press conference room.

She straightened his collar and adjusted his tie, and for a moment it was like it used to be when they first met. The excitement of this charismatic man who treated her like she was the only one in the room, which of course they were at that moment.

He kissed her gently like he used to, and she smiled despite herself. It held until he turned away, just. Then her face fell as reality came crashing back into her consciousness. She squared her shoulders and put her game-face on to follow him into the room. The press would smell any hint of weakness.

There were just a handful of reporters this time, most of them were down on the streets, covering the start of the protest. She saw Deanna Myers was watching her closely and nodded politely. How had she gotten back in? Ganelon was supposed to have taken care of that. Her blond pixie-cut hair and fitted suit were in sharp contrast to the older male reporters that made up the rest of the room. Sera couldn't help but feel a moment of solidarity with her. An island of the next generation in a sea of tired corruption. Except maybe she was part of that corrupt sea now.

"Good Morning," Bren said from the podium, and Sera forced her eyes back to him.

"Today our citizens are gathering on the streets to tell us how much they care about getting the Librarian algorithm right. That's exactly what I care most about as secretary for literary safety, and today I add my voice to theirs as I announce a commission of inquiry into the recent breach of the Literary Safety System. I am pleased to advise that Senator Bob McKay has accepted the position of chair..."

Sera tuned out as he carried on. He was sticking to the script for once and she'd read it so many times last night that she could have recited it from memory. She watched the faces of the journalists. As expected, the staid older reporters were nodding along in approval. Deanna Myers looked like she could barely stay seated. She didn't have long to wait to start her questions.

"Secretary, how will you make sure the commission isn't just another whitewash?" she asked.

"The people on the streets today are asking for an inquiry, and I'm proud to deliver on that request. Recorded rates of depression have dropped 30 percent since the Librarian algorithm was brought in, and together we can make sure that trend continues," Bren replied, eyes already searching for a safer question.

Deanna jumped in again before the others could speak up— "What do you say to the many researchers that have shown those with depression no longer seek treatment due to the stigma of censorship?"

Bren laughed, "Let the others get a word in, Ms Myers. It's not all about you."

Sera watched the other journalists snicker to themselves and raise their hands to ask their own questions. Her mouth tightened in annoyance. Bren wasn't showing the same respect anymore. He would never have responded like that last year, no matter how annoying the question.

"Do you have any leads on the suspected criminal Virginia Wright yet?" another journalist asked.

"I'm glad you asked, Steve. We're definitely closing in. We're asking the public to please keep an eye out at the protest today, as she may try to make an appearance. If you see anything suspicious, call the police immediately. With your help, we can catch her."

Sera's phone started vibrating and she looked at the screen—unknown number. She looked over at Bren. He had the questions covered. She wasn't needed right now. She quietly opened the door and slipped out into the corridor.

"Hello. Sera Olsen speaking," she said, once the door was closed.

"Ms Olsen. I saw the secretary speaking just now. I have information on Virginia Wright." The voice speaking was a man's, perhaps in his thirties or forties, and muffled as if he was trying hard to avoid being overheard.

"Any information needs to go to the police," Sera said.

"That's not an option. If you want to find her, you should check out the old post office building on the corner of Grange and Fifth Avenue."

He hung up just as Bren came out through the door.

"Well, that went well, apart from Myers. Is everything OK?" he asked.

Sera was slowly dropping the phone from her face while she processed the information.

"Yeah. Just my mother worried about my sister again," she lied.

Bren hugged her shoulders. "We'll get the restrictions back up soon and she can start healing again," he said.

Sera kept quiet as they made their way back to the offices.

The news reported fifteen thousand people at the protest, but the announcement of the commission had taken most of the sting out of it. Poll numbers were on the rise again and coverage of the commission's details slowly pushed out the images of people marching.

Sera had barely slept in days, and that phone call was still preying on her mind. Who had called her? Was it a test from Ganelon? Was it too late to tell the police now? Did she even want to?

Matty had been busy with his readers in the corner, releasing a deluge of Librarian-generated stories about commissions exposing the criminal underworld and the heroic politicians that stood up for victims of crime. Ganelon's algorithms stitching together the most popular snippets of prose into new narratives; the sentences that the cameras on people's readers had shown made their eyes dilate and their breath quicken in excitement. She couldn't believe the press hadn't picked up on it. Ms Myers at least would be having a fit.

She'd carefully avoided involving herself in any of Matty's work. Especially the stories that were transferred directly to Bren's reader for Grace. Which is why she was so surprised when she picked up her phone later in the week to hear Grace's quavering voice on the other end.

"Serafina? Can we talk? Alone?"

Sera glanced over at Matty at his desk. He wasn't obviously listening, but she knew he heard everything.

"Of course. Text me the details," she said, hoping Grace would understand why she wasn't speaking clearer.

"Eight p.m. this evening at The Coffee Shack on Fifth," Grace said, before hanging up.

Sera put the phone down and went back to her emails as if nothing had happened. Was it a coincidence that Grace wanted to meet three blocks down from where the anonymous tip-off had told her to find Virginia Wright? Or was Grace just trying to meet her somewhere she knew they were not going to run into anyone from the office? That part of town was run-down. Not somewhere she really wanted to walk around by herself at night.

Sera made sure Matty and Bren were occupied before she left the office that night, claiming another family dinner as her excuse. She even walked the entire way to her mother's in case she was being followed, slipping out the back entrance to the apartment building before anyone might be able to circle around to check.

She was fifteen minutes early to The Coffee Shack, but as she looked for a space to sit down with her steaming cup, she noticed a woman in the corner whose face was obscured by the hood of her jacket. Grace was already there.

Sera put her drink down on the table first, and Grace jumped at the clink of the china. That wasn't a good sign. Sera positioned herself with her back to the wall so Grace could look at her without showing her face to the rest of the café.

"Thanks for meeting me," Grace whispered.

"No problem. What's up?"

"I guess you know about...me and Brenton, already?" she muttered.

Sera looked down at her tea, breathing in the scent of soothing peppermint. Her adrenaline had spiked as soon as she saw Grace's hunched form and heard her shaking voice. What the hell had happened?

She looked back up at Grace again. "Yeah. It's my job to know."

Grace tilted her head to the side and a hint of her usual confidence returned as she said— "But your position with him is more than just a job, isn't it? I've seen the way he looks at you when he thinks I'm not paying attention."

Sera stared back at her.

"Are you here to threaten me?" she asked, keeping her voice steady.

"No! No. Not threaten. I just need to know you understand."

"I understand," Sera said, finally.

"Does he send you stories? Does he… act them out?" Her voice had lost its volume again.

Grace's eyes were firmly on the table, her cheeks flushed. Sera sighed and leaned back. So, Grace obviously hadn't been involved in setting Bren up. She was just another 'innocent' victim.

"No. We have a boundary. We have to work together," she said. But even as she said it, she wondered if it was still true.

"Have you seen them? The stories?"

"Only a little. I told him I didn't want anything to do with it," Sera replied.

Grace nodded and seemed to be gathering herself together. She sat up straighter in her chair, raising her chin.

"It was exciting at first. But it's gone too far."

She pulled her sleeve back and showed Sera the faint trace of rope burns around her wrists. Sera winced. It was worse than she'd thought if he was leaving marks on another man's wife.

"Did you tell him to stop?" she asked, softly.

Grace shook her head. Sera watched the tremble in her hand as she pulled her sleeve back down to cover her wrist.

"No. But I told him I'm not going to meet him again," she said.

"That sounds like a good decision."

Sera reached out to squeeze Grace's hand that had dropped beneath the table.

Grace replied so quietly that Sera had to strain to hear her. "He said he'll show Bob the video if I don't meet him again. I need your help. Please? He'll listen to you."

Sera swore to herself. What was wrong with him? She might have fooled herself into thinking he would listen to her last week. But now she wasn't so sure. She looked at Grace's face, the tears brimming in her eyes.

"I can try," she said.

Grace stood up to leave. Sera only just heard her murmured "Thank you," as she left.

Sera walked home past the abandoned building on Grange and Fifth. She stood across the street from it, staring at the darkened windows and wondering who might be staring back. As she turned to carry on, she ran into someone. The impact twisted her body as they slammed her shoulder. She hadn't even realised anyone was there. They carried on as if nothing had happened.

She reached into her pocket, feeling for the reassurance of her phone in case she needed to call for help. Only there was a piece of paper in there now, too.

She looked around in surprise, searching for the now-disappeared figure. They were nowhere to be seen. She held the note up to the streetlight to read it:

When you realise you're on the wrong side, give us a call—Gini.
The digits of a cell phone number were written underneath.

Sera looked around again, searching the vacant night. Then she tucked the note back in her pocket and ran the whole way home. Her mind spun as she realised the tip-off must have been arranged by Virginia Wright herself. A test. And when she hadn't called the police, she'd reached out again.

The next morning, she sat at her keyboard staring at the screen without typing a thing. She'd promised Grace she would try. She had to keep that promise.

She looked over at Matty, studiously bent over his readers like always. She would need all the help she could get. If she didn't have him onside, she wouldn't get anywhere.

"Matty?"

He looked up, a little surprised, and turned to face her. "Yes, Sera?"

"We have a small problem we need to manage."

He got up and shifted his chair to sit opposite her. "I'm listening."

"Your stories. The ones for the secretary, personally. They were a little too successful. The lady in question wants them to stop. Wants it all to stop."

Matty's eyes searched her face, inspecting her. "You've spoken to her directly? This isn't something else on your part?"

Sera frowned at the suggestion she was being jealous. "She was quite clear about it. The secretary is being… overenthusiastic. He won't let her go."

"Where's the problem, exactly?"

Sera sighed in exasperation. "There's only so much blackmail to go around, and this one is too far," she snapped.

"You think she might go public? As you know, it doesn't usually go well for the woman in that scenario," he warned.

"I think, between us, we can reign him in without anyone needing to even contemplate going public."

"I'll look into it," Matty said.

Sera watched him warily as he returned to his desk. What exactly was he going to look at? She needed a better idea of what he'd been up to. She logged onto her computer as Bren and opened the file of Matty's stories that she'd been avoiding looking at.

Along with the stories themselves, there were statistical reports on the balance of content in the reader database, and how it was shifting. She felt slightly ill at the trendline for "conservative morals". The next graph broke it down even further. She'd had no idea how widespread it went, well beyond the literary safety messaging they'd discussed with her.

She flicked through the series of stories that had gone to Grace. No wonder the poor woman was terrified. Each one was shadier than the last and there wasn't even a modicum of effort to imply consent in the most recent. Ganelon Inc. had nudged Bren further and further down this path. Or maybe he'd always been like that. She pressed ice-cold hands to her burning cheeks, hoping Matty wouldn't notice.

There was another folder tucked away in those files as well, labelled 'research'. She opened it up. It contained emails from the state scientists working on the literary safety programme. They raised concerns about the decline in reporting of depression that Deanna had asked about at the press conference. They also talked about increasing severity of mental illness symptoms presenting from those reporting "loss of autonomy" due to censorship. She'd heard the reports, of course. But no-one had told her their own scientists held the same concerns.

She looked up the date of the last complaint. They'd come through every month until three months ago when the chief medical officer had retired. She held her breath as she searched for details of his retirement. All she found was a recent news article:

Former Chief Medical Officer George Winten has been unable to be contacted to present evidence to the commission. Mr Winten is believed to have retired overseas.

Sera drew in a shaky breath and remembered Palmer's words—rumours of staff who had disappeared. Staff from their own agency. She quietly photographed each screen with her phone, making sure her hands were out of sight from Matty's desk. She couldn't afford there being a record of any file transfer. Then she stood up and knocked on Bren's door, not waiting for him to answer it. He looked up from his desk as she shut the door behind her.

"Why didn't you tell me about the complaints from the medical officers?" she asked.

Bren stood up and came around to perch on his desk in front of her, putting them eye-to-eye.

"I didn't want to upset you. I know what the Librarian program means to you," he said.

"Because I need to be 'protected' like I'm some kind of child?"

The words were barely out of her mouth when she realised they were exactly what her sister had said to her. She could almost feel the click in her mind like a dislocated joint being snapped back into place. The realisation that she had made a terrible mistake. What had she helped do to the world?

"Not protected like a child. Protected like my lover, sweetheart," Bren said.

He pulled her into his arms and her mind was reeling so fast she let him. Did he know about the disappearance of the medical officer? He must do. How much had he been keeping from her?

The phone rang on the desk, saving her from having to figure out how to extract herself. Bren sighed as he listened to the receptionist. He turned back to Sera as he hung the phone up, kissing her again.

"The journalist is here to do that interview. Are you OK?"

She forced herself to smile at him, placing a hand on his chest as if she was still interested in something more when really it was just so she could push him away if she needed to.

"Yeah, I'm fine. You know how I get when you don't tell me about stuff I might need to manage. I'll make sure we've got a communication plan ready if they track George down. You need to tell me this stuff!" she said.

Bren grinned. "Yes, ma'am. You can scold me later."

Sera pulled away and went to fetch the journalist. All she really wanted to do was take a long hot shower. She knew it wouldn't wash the guilt from her hands, though.

CHAPTER 7

Sera could feel Matty's eyes watching her whenever she was in her office. Bren must have told him she knew about the research. She'd memorised Gini's number and burned the slip of paper. She couldn't risk being found with it. Her sister's game-piece sat on her desk by her computer, a constant reminder of the damage she had caused by helping these people.

She kept replaying the last year over in her head. Trying to figure out how she hadn't noticed what was going on. The only answer was that she hadn't noticed because she hadn't wanted to. Bren was charming and she had felt like a full-time saviour. A champion for all the troubled kids like her sister. What a joke. She couldn't even apologise to her, because what if Ganelon realised she no longer supported the system?

What would they do to her if they thought she was a risk?

She was so distracted, it was two days before she could bring herself to check in with Grace. She rang her number and it went straight to voicemail. She looked up Bob's calendar and found a social engagement the following month. At lunchtime, from the relative anonymity of the city streets, she rang the senator's personal assistant.

"Hi. It's Renee here from the Daisy Trust, I just wanted to check the RSVP for next month. Will the senator be bringing anyone with him? Will his wife be attending?" Sera said.

The assistant didn't miss a beat. "No, just him. His wife is overseas at the moment."

Sera shivered in the sun's heat as she ended the call. She was sure Grace would have mentioned if she was travelling. She would never have reached out for help if she could just leave. Overseas. Just like the former chief medical officer.

She rang Gini's number.

"Serafina?" came the woman's voice over the phone.

"Yes. I've come to that realisation," she said.

"Meet me in an hour. Same place as before."

Sera was still three blocks away from the meet when a hand reached out and pulled her into an alleyway, covering her mouth to keep her from screaming.

"Quiet. It's me," said a woman's voice.

Sera turned around to see a woman in a bright red jacket and stiletto heels. Not at all what she'd been expecting from a fugitive on the run, or from the photos she'd been given of ex-Detective Virginia Wright.

Gini saw her looking and shrugged her shoulders. "I don't have the luxury of looking like myself anymore. How do I know I can trust you?"

Sera stared at the gruff woman standing before her. She could see the outline of a gun tucked in a belt-holster under her jacket. Would she use it if she didn't help her? Did it even matter at this point?

"You don't. If I help you, will you take Ganelon down?" Sera said.

Gini looked surprised. "What did they do to piss you off so much? I'm certainly doing my best to take them down."

Sera stood in the alley, poised on the edge of what felt like a ravine. She didn't have anyone else to turn to. She'd read the reports about Gini. She'd been a good cop before the incident. And she was smart enough to have avoided capture for the last month. She was her best chance. Sera got her phone out of her pocket.

"Good enough. I'm going to transfer some photos to you. Lines of investigation. If you publish them, Ganelon will probably make me disappear. They're already watching me. They may well do it anyway," she said

Gini accepted the photos and looked over them as she spoke. "Shit. This is good stuff. We can look into this medical officer guy. See if we can find him. What happened to change your mind? They must know you're not happy. Why haven't they made you disappear already?"

Sera shrugged. "Maybe they still have a use for me. Maybe they think I'll stay on the secretary's leash. Who knows. You need to find Grace McKay, too. She disappeared two days ago."

"Are they covering something up? Did she know something?" Gini asked.

Shame made Sera looked away. "They were helping seduce her for the secretary and it went bad. She wanted out."

"That must have been awkward for you."

Sera glared at her. Did everyone know about her and Bren? She sighed. "I guess you've been in touch with Palmer?"

"That's how we got your number. He said he thought you might be approachable."

"Are you going to go public with that?" Sera asked with dull eyes, pointing at the phone.

Gini shook her head. "Not yet. We look after our own. We'll get you out before we do. Palmer and Myers will help me investigate. Between us, we'll find something we can pin on them."

"Deanna Myers?" Sera asked, horrified.

"Yes. What did you think we were going to do? Can't go public without someone from the media. You still in?" she asked, holding out her hand.

Sera stared at it and then reached out to clasp it in her own. "Yeah. I'm in."

"Good. We need you to hang in there. You're our only insider in this. With you in the secretary's office, we can stay out of police reach and you can tell us where we need to look. You're the key. Without you, I don't think we can get there."

Sera nodded. She was sick with anxiety, but a weight had also lifted off her. She was helping people for real now. She could save actual lives, if Grace was even still alive.

She was partway back to her office when she got the call from her mother.

"Riley's in the hospital! They found her with an empty bottle of pills. They can't wake her up," her mother's panicked voice said.

"I'm on my way!" Sera cried, breaking into a run.

Sera sat by Riley's hospital bed, clutching tightly to her hand. She'd sent her mom home to rest at ten p.m., but she couldn't tear herself away. Her eyes watched her chest rise and fall. Her breath wheezing through too-pale lips. The doctors had pumped her stomach, but she was still in a coma. They didn't know when she might wake up.

She rested her forehead on her sister's clammy hand, feeling her face press into the scratchy wool blanket. She relished the discomfort. It was more than she deserved. Her sister had never taken a pill in her life. That was part of the struggle they'd had, she wouldn't take anything for the depression. This overdose had Ganelon's fingerprints all over it.

She must have fallen asleep like that because she woke hours later to a firm hand on her shoulder. She looked up with aching red-rimmed eyes at Bren standing above her. She was still groggy from sleep. He pulled her up into his arms and held her tightly.

"Oh, Sera. I'm so sorry. We'll make sure she gets the best treatment. I wish we'd managed to get the restrictions back up faster so we could have avoided this," he said.

Sera stood stiff in his arms. Was he really going to try and pretend her sister had done this to herself? Who the hell did he think he was? Then her brain caught up. Virginia needed her. Grace needed her. Her sister needed her. She needed to make them pay and she couldn't do that if she joined her sister in a hospital bed, or worse.

"She wouldn't let me take her reader. I tried," she said.

"I know you did your best, sweetheart," Bren said, kissing her head.

Sera struggled to find the words that would keep him unsuspecting. The words that would keep them all safe a while longer.

"We need to stop this happening to anyone else," she said.

"I'll call the Ganelon team first thing tomorrow morning. No more delays. We need to get those restrictions back up," Bren said.

Sera looked up at him with tears in her eyes. "What did I do to deserve you?" she said, and she meant it with every ounce of her being. Had she really been that evil?

Bren smiled at her kindly, oblivious to what she really meant. "You need to go home and get some sleep. How about I come stay with you tonight? You shouldn't be alone."

Sera couldn't bring herself to answer. She looked over at her sister's face. She owed her. She had to be strong for her. She reached out and grabbed her bag from the side table. Then she turned to Bren and took his hand.

"Yes. I need you to love me," she said.

Bren swept her out the door.

Honesty was the best way to lie. That's how they did it at the press conferences all the time. She did need him to love her. Because then he wouldn't see the axe until it fell. And with any luck, Ganelon wouldn't see it either.

Love is a compact of fire. She could use it to burn it all down.

Enjoy what you read? Please review!
Hell is Empty is the next Censored City novelette.

You can subscribe to Melanie's newsletter at:
www.MelanieHardingShaw.com

ABOUT THE AUTHOR

Melanie Harding-Shaw is a speculative fiction writer, policy geek, and mother-of-three from Wellington, New Zealand. Her short fiction has appeared in publications like Daily Science Fiction and The Arcanist, and she was a finalist for Best Short Story in the 2019 Sir Julius Vogel Awards.

You can find her at:
www.MelanieHardingShaw.com
Facebook @MelanieHardingShawWriter
Twitter @MelHardingShaw